One day in May, Mr. Toffy brought a big man to see Samuel.

'Meet Louey!' said Mr. Toffy, 'Louey owns a circus in America, and he wants you to go there and work for him'.

'How do you feel about it kid?' asked Louey.

Samuel had seen a lot of America on TV, and knew all about it. The cowboys, the wagons, the prairies, all those lovely open spaces with not a crowd in sight.

'I'd love to go, sir,' answered Samuel (politely, as usual).

In no time at all, Samuel had packed his trunk (his SUITCASE trunk, not his NOSE trunk) and he and Louey were strapped in their seats in a Jumbo Jet.

'Hmmmmm,' thought Samuel, 'just the right plane for an elephant.'

After seven hours, the jet landed with a bump.

'Here we are, little old New York!' said Louey.

'Wonder how he talks without taking his cigar out of his mouth?' pondered Samuel.

Once out of the plane, Samuel took his first look at America. He was HORRIFIED.

'Get a load of that!' drawled Louey, waving his cigar about.

Samuel got a load of that.

The tall buildings leaned over him.

The cars screamed at him.

Even the air seemed to jostle and shove.

And the people! There were hundreds of people, pushing and crowding, and staring at the little elephant.

Ignoring Louey's shouts, Samuel began to run. And a frightened Samuel was the fastest elephant in the world.

Having escaped the towering, clamouring city, Samuel ran and ran, until he was puffed out.

'I must find a quiet place to sit down!' he gasped. 'Even a fast elephant can't run for ever'.

He stopped and looked around him.

He was in a railway yard.

In the distance, the city glared at him. Running to a huge train, he clambered into the darkest wagon and pulled the door closed. Once inside, Samuel grew calmer. All was quiet.

The little elephant looked around him.
In another corner, sitting on a pile of straw, was a ladybird. Samuel went to sit by her. (He wasn't as shy with insects.)
'I'm English,' he announced, 'and soon I'll be back there when this train gets going!'
'Poor dope,' thought the ladybird, 'he doesn't know the Atlantic Ocean is between here and England.'
Just then, the train began to clank as it moved away.
A contented Samuel dozed off.

Samuel awoke with a start. The train had rattled to a halt.

'This is as far as we go, son!' drawled the ladybird. 'By the way, my name's Delia, and I'm in Florida visiting my sister'.

'FLORIDA . . . ! Good gosh,' gasped Samuel, 'is Florida anywhere near England?'

'Don't think so son,' grinned Delia, as she crawled away dragging a big yellow suitcase.

Samuel climbed down after her and looked around. He seemed to be in the middle of nowhere.

Samuel was alone at last. He was in some kind of desert.

He amused himself by building sandcastles, then throwing stones at them.

'This is the life,' he said to himself happily.

After a while, he began to feel peckish and, as elephants have big tummies, he was soon feeling VERY peckish.

Shading his eyes from the sun with a huge foot, he searched the landscape for a cafe, or something.

In the distance there was a very tall tower. Samuel plodded towards it.

When he got nearer, Samuel could make out what the tower was.

'Wow!' he breathed, 'a rocket.'

Suddenly the peace and quiet was shattered. From all directions, cars and buses full of people appeared and made for the rocket. Taking fright for the second time, the shy little elephant began to run.

The people were crowding all around, and Samuel only had one place to hide.

Without a moment's hesitation, he shinned up a little ladder and fell into the rocket. CLUNK went the thick door behind him.

Mopping his brow with relief, Samuel sat down.
RIGHT ON A BIG RED BUTTON.
With a thunderous WHOOSH, the rocket began to shake.
Samuel fainted!
Outside the clouds whizzed by, and then the earth fell
away. Everything was black.
When Samuel woke up, the rocket had landed. He
staggered to a window and an amazing sight greeted him.
The sky was black, and the land was white. Round the
rocket stood a ring of animals. He was on another planet,
but he saw that the animals were like the ones on Earth.

Jumping down out of the rocket, Samuel greeted them. 'How do you do?' he said politely. 'Who are you all?'
'We're all from EARTH,' answered a Hippo.
'Some of us are from America, some of us from Russia, and some from China. We all have one thing in common, we are all shy! Somehow or other, we all hid in those pointed silver things like yours,' he pointed at the rocket, 'and whizz, bang, wallop, here we are!'

A bear called Ivan took Samuel by the arm.
'Welcome to our home,' he said. 'We love it here. We've built cages to live in, we make jelly and cakes, and we've lots of games to play. Best of all, there's no crowds to stare at us. PLEASE STAY!'
Samuel smiled, and thought to himself, 'I don't see how I can leave!'
Then he smiled a bigger smile and thought, 'If everyone else is shy like me I won't need to run away.' So he said to Ivan, 'I like it here already. By the way, I'm Samuel.'
Funny, but Samuel didn't feel shy any more.